THE
BUMBLE BEAST

By Harriet Grey

A PARACHUTE PRESS BOOK

A PARACHUTE PRESS BOOK
Parachute Press, Inc.
156 Fifth Avenue
New York, NY 10010

Creative Consultant: Cheryl Saban.

With special thanks to Cheryl Saban, Debi Young, Ban Pryor, and
Sherry Stack.

Printed in the U.S.A.
August 1994
ISBN: 0-938753-84-3
B C D E F G H I J

PROLOGUE

Evil forces beware. Five ordinary teenagers are about to morph into—the Mighty Morphin Power Rangers.

Their incredible powers come from Zordon, a good wizard trapped in another dimension. Zordon has given each teenager a

magic coin—a Power Morpher—
and super strength drawn from
the spirits of the dinosaurs.

When things get really tough,
the Power Rangers call upon their
Dinozords—giant robots they
drive into battle.

Power Rangers, dinosaur spirits, and amazing robots—together
these incredible forces protect
the Earth.

So—get ready. *It's morphin
time!*

CHAPTER 1

It was the last period of the day at Angel Grove High School and Ms. Appleby, the science teacher, was handing back everybody's corrected tests. When she reached Billy's desk, she paused for a moment.

"Here you are, Billy," she said,

giving him his exam.

Billy took it, prepared to smile at his usual A-plus, but then he gazed in horror at the bright red B written at the top of the page. "I don't believe it," he gasped loudly. "I got a B!"

"Remember," Ms. Appleby told the class, "only those with the top grades will be invited to join the Young Scientists of America Club. Tomorrow is the final test. So study hard."

The school bell rang and the students began filing out of the room, but Billy didn't move. He was the smartest kid in the class, and he *never* got anything but A's.

Kimberly, Jason, Zack, and Trini

all exchanged glances as Billy slowly stood up and shuffled toward them. The five teenagers were best friends, but they shared more than friendship. When they weren't busy with school, the group used their secret super-powers to protect the planet. Whenever evil forces tried to take over the Earth, the five friends turned into—the Mighty Morphin Power Rangers!

"I'm most perplexed," Billy said, sounding stunned. "I've never received a B before!" The letter B echoed through his head over and over. His blue eyes widened behind his glasses as he stared miserably down at the big

B on his test paper.

"It's okay, Billy," Jason said, winking at him. Jason was tall and handsome, with thick brown hair. Usually he had a way of making people feel better. "It's not a big deal—it's only one test."

"Don't sweat it, man," Zack added, heartily giving Billy a pat on the arm. "A B's not so bad." With that, the dark-haired teen tried to cheer Billy up with a new hip-hop move—but it didn't work.

"Yeah," Kimberly agreed. She smiled at Billy as she pulled her shoulder-length brown hair back into a ponytail. "If B's were really bad, I'd be in big trouble—I get B's all the time!"

"Perhaps, Kimberly," Billy said dully. "But I never do, and I've been working so hard."

Trini brushed her black bangs away from her pretty face and then draped her arm gracefully around Billy's shoulders. She had on a yellow sweater over flower-print leggings. "You did your best, Billy. That's all any of us can do."

Just then, Bulk and Skull, the two biggest bullies at Angel Grove High School, strutted over to the five friends.

"Tough luck about the B, geek!" Bulk snickered. He looked as goofy as usual, wearing a brightly colored shirt under a black leather jacket. "*B* stands for bad, don't you know?"

Bulk turned to his buddy, Skull, for support.

"Yeah, *B* stands for Bulk, too, doesn't it?" Skull said with a chuckle.

Bulk scowled at him, and Skull laughed harder.

"Bug off, Bulk," Jason said.

"Yeah," Kimberly agreed. "Leave Billy alone."

Bulk and Skull both smirked and made their way toward the door.

"See ya, wouldn't want to BE ya!" Bulk yelled back.

The letter *B!B!B!* echoed through Billy's mind again. He sank back against the wall, covering his face with his hands.

He was never going to live this down!

Far away, in a fortress on the moon, someone was living it up. It was Rita Repulsa. She had been spying on the Power Rangers through her magic telescope, and she always gloated whenever anything bad happened to them.

Now she stormed around her balcony, gesturing wildly with her long, black fingernails. Rita loved everything pointy. She wore a crown with two tall points, and the sleeves of her red and gold cloak were pointy, too.

Her chief warrior, Goldar, paced

next to her. His shiny red eyes glowed almost as brightly as his suit of gold armor.

"B, B, B," Rita cackled over and over. Then she stopped with a shriek. "Ha! That's it—a bee! What a brilliant idea!" She swept over to the workshop where Finster, her head monster-maker, invented his cruel creations.

"Finster! Make me a nasty stinger bee!" she ordered. "A bee to destroy the world!"

"Right away, O Wicked One," Finster replied. A smile spread across his pale and droopy face. He picked up a gooey handful of clay and quickly started to mold a new monster. He couldn't wait to see his new monsters come to life once they popped out of his magic Monster-matic machine. This was very nasty work, and he enjoyed every minute of it.

"Make it a bee monster that shoots poison with its deadly stingers!" Goldar instructed, rubbing his hands together with glee. "Then we can finally settle the score with those Power Rangers once and for all!"

CHAPTER 2

Billy was still very upset about his test as he walked down the hall to his locker with his friends. The janitor had just mopped up the corridor and arranged orange cones around the damp floor, along with a sign that read: Wet Floor. Caution!

"Hey, man, don't take it so hard," Zack said. "Maybe an A-plus just wasn't meant to BE."

Billy groaned at Zack's comment and stuck his head deep inside his open locker. Zack looked guilty and shrugged an apology to the others.

"Why don't you come shoot a few baskets to take your mind off your grade?" Jason suggested.

Billy shook his head, his mood as blue as his overalls. "No, thanks," he said. "I appreciate your efforts, but acceptance into the Young Scientists of America Club is very important to me. All of the best students in the country are in the club, and I would very much like to compete with them. I'd better go to the youth center and study."

"I'll go, too," Trini volunteered. "I can quiz you."

"Thank you," Billy said. "That would be most helpful."

As they all stood there in the hall, Bulk and Skull strutted up. Bulk was chowing down a sand- wich that was dripping with honey—and making a real mess all over the freshly washed floor.

"To BE or not to BE!" Bulk teased.

Billy flinched.

"Oops! Did I say something wrong?" Bulk asked. He bit into his disgusting sandwich and honey gushed all over his hands. "A nice, gooey snack," he added, then paused. "By the way, Skull, who makes honey?"

"Would that *be* a *bee*?" Skull guessed.

"You're right!" Bulk shouted. He nudged Billy with a big, sticky elbow. "Oh, sorry, geek. You just can't stay away from that *B* word, can you, B-B-Billy?"

"Take off, Bulk," Jason said firmly.

Bulk and Skull laughed and strolled away. Neither of them noticed the Wet Floor sign, or the mop and bucket nearby. They both slipped and ended up in a drenched heap on the floor.

"I guess you're all washed up now, eh, Bulk?" Zack joked.

The five friends laughed.

Bulk just grumbled, and he and Skull sloshed noisily away.

"So," Jason said, bouncing his basketball a few times, "are you sure you won't change your mind, Billy?"

"I'd better study," Billy said reluctantly. The final test was the next day, and this time, he was going to make sure he'd get nothing less than an A!

Up in the gloomy fortress on the moon, Rita and Goldar hovered near the Monster-matic. They waited impatiently for

Finster's newest monster to be finished.

"Wait 'til those power brats see *my* A student!" Rita screeched.

Finster peered into the big machine. "Here it comes," he said proudly. "My greatest beast ever—the Grumble Bee!"

He opened the cover of the big Monster-matic, and the Grumble Bee tumbled out.

The freshly baked creature flapped its wings, slowly at first, and then so rapidly that it made an earsplitting buzz sound. Rita and Goldar covered their ears.

"The noise can be heard for miles," Finster bragged. "On Earth, they won't know what hit them! And its wings are powerful enough to knock down anything— or anyone—that gets in its way."

"The Grumble Bee will teach the Power Rangers a thing or two, Your Evilness!" Goldar said happily. "And after our bee is done with them, it will destroy the world!"

Meanwhile, in the Angel Grove Youth Center, Billy and Trini arranged piles of their school books on a table. Trini threw her long black hair back over her shoulders and began to read from an encyclopedia.

"This says that the bee is the highest form of insect, belonging to the order called Hymenoptera," she said with a frown.

Billy clapped one hand to his forehead. "That's one of the answers I missed! I can't believe I blew the test on a *bee* question."

Trini lowered the book. "Do you know what it means?"

"Certainly," Billy said, feeling smart for the first time in more than an hour. "It's a name that defines a particular kind of insect...such as a bee."

"You're amazing, Billy," Trini said admiringly.

Billy looked pleased. "Keep reading," he urged.

While Billy and Trini studied, Jason, Zack, and Kimberly shot baskets in the park.

"I hope Billy doesn't wear himself out from too much studying," Zack remarked.

"I know what you mean," Kimberly agreed. "Getting a B on a test is nothing to be ashamed of."

Jason snagged the ball from Zack and dribbled a few steps away. "But don't forget," he reminded them, "Billy's a straight A student. For him, getting a B is a letdown."

Zack stole the ball back and flicked it through the hoop. "And getting into that Young Scientists of America Club is really important to him," he said.

Jason and Kimberly nodded

thoughtfully, and then they all dove for the rebound.

As Rita spied on the teenagers through her telescope up on the moon, she fumed. She hated to see them having fun!

"Once those Power Rangers meet my Grumble Bee, they'll never play and laugh again!" she yelled. Then she scowled and jabbed a black fingernail at Finster. He was still perfecting the poison for his new monster's stingers, and Rita was losing patience.

"What's taking you so long?" she shouted.

"The poison is not deadly

enough, Wicked Queen," Finster replied, hurrying.

Rita whirled around to glare at Goldar. "So, what are you waiting for?" she shrieked in a voice that could break glass. "*Do* something to make those Power Rangers miserable until the bee is ready!"

"Yes, Mistress of Madness! As you wish," Goldar said with a bow. "The Putties and I will go down for a little visit and soften up those puny Rangers." The Putties were mindless clay fighting creatures that Rita used in her war against the Power Rangers.

"Do it now!" Rita screamed. "Teach those Power Rangers a lesson they'll never forget!"

Swish! Kimberly had just made a basket when she heard a familiar gurgling *whoosh!*

She turned around and saw the Putty Patrol flipping onto the court. "Oh, great," she said grumpily. "Putties at mid-court."

"Spread out!" Jason ordered,

moving into a ready stance. "Let's take them!"

Zack, Kimberly, and Jason launched into a karate fight with the Putties, kicking and dodging and flipping.

"Take that!" Zack yelled, side kicking two of the Putties. "Ki-yaaah!"

Kimberly backflipped and landed both feet smack into a Putty's stomach. Jason tossed the ball at a Putty, then tackled him to the ground.

Just as the teenagers were about to finish them off, Goldar suddenly appeared with a new group of Putties. The Power Rangers did their best to fight back, but this time they were out-numbered.

"You think you're pretty smart, Power Rangers," Goldar smirked. "But trust me—this class has just begun. I'm sure you'll enjoy the lesson!"

Goldar whipped out a strange-looking gold rope and tossed it to several of the Putty Patrollers. They quickly surrounded the Power Rangers and tied the rope tightly around them.

"Hey!" Kimberly protested. "Cut it out, putty-brain!"

"This magic rope will keep you out of our way," Goldar said with a nasty smile. "Enjoying the class so far? Ha-ha-ha!"

The teens struggled against the rope. But the magic strands shimmered eerily with electricity, creating a force too powerful to escape.

"You can't get away with this, Goldar," Jason warned, twisting as hard as he could.

"I already have!" Goldar said triumphantly. "You failed *this* test, Power Rangers!" He snapped his fingers, and the Putties instantly swooped back to his side. "We've created a monstrous bee, power brats! It's our best monster yet. This time, you cannot stop us."

The teens fought with all their might, but the ropes only glowed and fastened around them more and more tightly.

"Our evil bee will destroy the world!" Goldar added, laughing. Then he and the Putties disappeared.

The three Power Rangers were helpless—caught in Goldar's trap!

Several thousand miles away, at a secret Command Center, a little robot, Alpha 5, was in a panic. Alpha gazed into the viewing globe and saw the freshly baked Grumble Bee. It landed in Angel Grove, waving a pair of huge stingers that dripped with poison.

"Aye-yi-yi-yi-yi!" Alpha cried. "We must contact Jason and the others, Zordon."

Zordon's pale face wavered in a column of eerie green light. The expression on his face grew worried as he watched the scenes on the viewing globe.

"We cannot reach Jason now," Zordon said in his deep voice.

The brightly glowing crystal ball now showed Jason, Zack, and Kimberly wriggling to free themselves from the magic rope.

"Oh, no!" Alpha said. "They're really tied up! What do we do, Zordon?"

"Contact Billy and Trini immediately," Zordon commanded.

The little robot nodded. "Right away, Zordon," he answered.

Billy and Trini were still hunched over their science books in the youth center when they heard their wrist communicators beep. They glanced around to make sure no one was watching and then rushed to a quiet corner to respond.

"Yes, Zordon," Billy said softly into the speaker on his wristband.

"Teleport to the Command Center immediately!" Zordon told them.

"Affirmative, Zordon," Billy said, and clicked off.

Billy and Trini dashed out to the entrance hall. After checking to be sure that they were alone, they touched their teleporter buttons. Instantly they transported to the Command Center.

"What's happening, Zordon?" Billy asked.

Trini looked around. "Where's everyone else?"

"Your friends are being held by an electronic force inside Goldar's magic rope," Zordon explained. "Behold the viewing globe."

Billy and Trini turned to see an image of their friends struggling desperately on the basketball court.

"Oh, no!" Trini groaned.

"I haven't figured out how to free them yet," Alpha 5 said, as he hung his metal head sadly. "Oh, this is an awful mess!"

**Billy is upset about his science test grade.
"I've never received a B before!"**

**"Tough luck about the B, geek!" Bulk
snickers.**

Billy learns from Alpha that Goldar has trapped Jason, Kimberly, and Zack! *And* **Rita has created a new monster!**

Trini knows exactly what she and Billy have to do next. "It's morphin time!"

Billy calls upon the spirit of his ancient dinosaur. "Triceratops!"

"Saber-toothed Tiger!" cries Trini.

The Blue Ranger is ready to smash the new monster—the Grumble Bee!

"I'll help you buzz off, you hideous bumble beast," the Yellow Ranger cries.

Zack, Jason, and Kimberly escape and help fight the terrible creature!

The five friends ace two big challenges—Billy gets an A on his science test and the Grumble Bee is gone forever!

"We'll go to them right away," Billy said.

"Wait!" Zordon boomed. "There is a much more pressing problem, Power Rangers. Return your attention to the globe."

Trini and Billy looked, and couldn't believe their eyes. The viewing globe revealed a gigantic monster with bold yellow and black stripes and dangerous, sharp stingers. Its wide wings waved wildly as it lumbered up a hill in Angel Grove, obviously looking for trouble.

"Rita has created a monstrous bee that shoots deadly poison from its stingers," Zordon said. "Left alone, it could destroy humankind!"

"We have to stop it!" Trini said instantly.

"But…" Billy hesitated. "What about the others? We can't *leave* them there."

"Alpha is working on a solution to that problem," Zordon replied. "But you must head off Rita's monster *now!*"

Billy and Trini exchanged serious looks. They knew exactly what they had to do next.

"It's morphin time!" Trini cried.

CHAPTER 4

The air crackled with electricity as Trini and Billy raised their Power Morphers to the sky. Just as Zordon had taught them, they called upon the spirits of the ancient dinosaurs.

"Triceratops!" cried Billy.

"Saber-toothed Tiger!" cried Trini.

Now they stood dressed in shiny helmets and sleek jumpsuits—two powerful protectors. Then Trini the Yellow Ranger and Billy the Blue Ranger vanished, and reappeared in Angel Grove—face-to-face with the terrifying Grumble Bee! It was the most frightening insect they'd ever seen.

"We will not allow you to destroy the planet!" the Yellow Ranger shouted at the monster. "Leave—now!"

"No way, Power Rangerzzz," the Grumble Bee rumbled in a loud buzzing voice. "I've only just bee-gun."

Hundreds of glowing white

stingers shot out from its black hairy arms. The Yellow Ranger ducked, but the Blue Ranger was hit and fell to the ground.

A loud *bee-bee-bee* sound echoed through Billy's head, and he couldn't move.

The Yellow Ranger helped him up and the two charged at the beast.

Again the Grumble Bee fired its poisonous stingers. There was a loud explosion. The Blue Ranger crashed heavily to the ground.

Trini gasped. "Did you get hit, Billy? Are you okay?"

The Blue Ranger lay on the ground, dazed. "The stingers missed me, but that last blast really rocked me," he mumbled.

The monster shot a stinger barb at Trini, but she was too quick for it. She climbed swiftly up a tree, avoiding the shower of sparks and smoke. If she had to, she would fight by herself!

"I'll help you buzz off, you hideous bumble beast!" Trini called. "Hiii-yaah!" The Yellow Ranger leaped from the tree, and landed on the monster's chest. The force of her blow sent the Grumble Bee rolling down the hill.

"Come on, Billy, I'll set you up for the high flip!" Trini shouted. "Let's get rid of this creep!"

Billy rushed toward Trini, who cupped her hands so that she

could give him a big boost. He launched into a high gymnastic leap. But his karate kick fell short, and the Blue Ranger landed flat on his back.

Trini stared at him in surprise. "What happened?" she asked. "You've never missed that flip before."

"Sorry, Trini," Billy said, looking defeated. "I can't seem to get anything right today."

"Don't give up, Billy," the Yellow Ranger cried. "You can do it if you try! We must beat him! The fate of the world is on our shoulders!"

"You're right." Billy dragged himself up. "I'm ready."

"Watch *this,* Power Rangerzzz," Grumble Bee buzzed. "Now I'll show you my true power!" The monster began to beat its wings, creating a sound wave so piercing that the Power Rangers couldn't bear it.

"Oh, no!" Trini shrank down, clasping her arms around her yellow helmet. "My ears!"

"The sound is deafening!" Billy shouted. "We can't take this for long!"

The Grumble Bee laughed and created more ghastly sound waves with another fierce flap of its wings.

"It's getting worse!" Trini said. "We'd better teleport out of here."

"I agree," Billy answered. "We need some help!"

A second later the Blue and Yellow Rangers teleported back to the Command Center.

"Zordon, the ultrasonic buzz sound is too powerful," Billy said as they appeared in the Command Center. "We must locate the monster's weakness and destroy it!"

"Don't worry," Zordon said. "Alpha is creating a special weapon for that purpose."

Trini pointed at the viewing globe, which showed Jason, Zack, and Kimberly still caught inside the electronic rope. "What about the others?" she asked.

"We can't defeat the Grumble

Bee alone," Billy said. "We've got to free Kimberly, Zack, and Jason."

"Good luck, Power Rangers," Zordon called out as Billy and Trini teleported straight to the basketball court.

"Boy, am I glad to see you two," Jason said as Billy and Trini appeared before the tied-up teens.

Billy yanked on the rope with both hands, but he couldn't loosen it. Trini joined in, but even the two of them couldn't budge the tight coils an inch.

"Hurry up, please!" Kimberly begged.

"Come on," Zack urged them.

"Pull harder!"

Then Billy's communicator beeped and Zordon's deep voice came through. "The situation has gotten worse. The Grumble Bee is getting ready to destroy the whole town. You and Trini must morph and battle the beast once again!"

"But how can we leave our friends here?" Trini asked.

"You've got to go," Jason said. "Don't worry about us. You and Billy have to stop the monster. Before it's too late!"

Trini and Billy morphed and teleported straight into battle with the deadly Grumble Bee.

"Ready for round two, Grumble Bee?" Trini asked. "Hiii-yaah!" she shouted and side kicked the mean monster.

The Grumble Bee rolled over, then bounced up, unleashing a wave of poisonous stingers.

The Yellow and Blue Rangers dodged and attacked again. But the Grumble Bee buzzed back up with a gleeful wave of its stingers.

"You have felt my sting, now feel the power of my poison!" the monster screamed. From its mouth it sprayed a yellow substance onto Billy. The Blue Ranger fell back, crying out in pain.

Trini dashed to help the fallen Ranger. "Oh, no! What *is* that stuff, Billy?"

"Stay back, Trini!" Billy warned as the yellow poison burned through his blue jumpsuit. "The venom is toxic—and it's melting a hole right through my suit!"

Trini swallowed. It was up to her to defeat the Grumble Bee—alone. "I hope Alpha can find a way to free the others," she said, and bravely launched a karate kick at the laughing Grumble Bee.

No matter what, she would *never* give up!

Inside the Command Center, Alpha fiddled with the buttons and dials on the control panel. He was trying as hard as he could to make a weapon to defeat the Grumble Bee—and free the other Power Rangers from Goldar's rope prison. Accidentally, he pulled a lever and pushed a button at the same time. Sparks flew everywhere, and he jumped back.

"Aye-yi-yi-yi-yi!" cried the little robot. "What have I done *now?*"

Next to him, the viewing globe crackled to life and he saw the rope fall away from Jason, Zack, and Kimberly as the electronic force weakened. The red lever and the blue button must have been the right combination!

"Good work, Alpha," Zordon praised the robot.

"We're free!" Jason exclaimed, raising his fists in victory.

Just then his communicator went off. "We read you, Zordon." Jason lifted his arm and spoke into his wrist speaker.

"Alpha dismantled the electronic force field," Zordon announced. "We're creating a weapon to destroy the Grumble Bee, but now you must morph and help Trini and Billy. They are in trouble."

Jason turned to the others. "Okay, guys," he shouted. "It's morphin time!"

They held up their Power Morphers to summon the spirits of the dinosaurs.

"Mastodon!" Zack cried, and morphed into the Black Ranger.

"Pterodactyl!" Kimberly cried, and morphed into the Pink Ranger.

"Tyrannosaurus!" Jason cried,

and morphed into the Red Ranger.

It was time to help their friends!

They teleported to the hill where Billy and Trini were struggling against the Grumble Bee—just as Rita's Putty Patrol joined the battle.

"Buzz off, bee!" Jason shouted as he landed a powerful punch to the beast's belly.

"Hey, losers!" Zack cried as he charged two Putties.

"Ki-yaaah!" Trini yelled as she karate chopped a Putty to the ground.

Two more Putties grabbed Zack.

"I'm not in the mood to fool around with you guys!" Zack

exclaimed. He backflipped and knocked them flat.

Trini karate kicked another Putty forcefully out of her way. "This will teach you to mess with us!" she yelled.

"Let me give you a hand, Trini," Kimberly, the Pink Ranger, said. She zipped at the Putties with a whirl of dazzling spins and kicks. "Try this, mud-putties!"

Overwhelmed by the Power Rangers, the beaten Putties disappeared. But Billy had been hit with another burst of poisonous venom. And the battle was far from over. The superheroes still had to face their deadly enemy, the Grumble Bee.

"End of lesson, Grumble Bee," Jason said. "It's over!"

"Not so fast," the monster said. "Here's *another* test for you!" The bee fired its stingers. As the Power Rangers dodged the darts, the beast flapped its monstrous wings. Blast after blast of ultra-sonic waves slammed the Power Rangers to the ground.

"What's that noise?" Jason cried out, paralyzed by the ear-splitting buzz.

"Whoa, this is loud," Zack groaned.

"Just hold your ears!" Trini yelled as loud as she could.

The Grumble Bee laughed crazily. "I've won!" it shouted.

"You fail the test! Ha-ha-ha! Your powers are *worthless!*"

While the buzzing Grumble Bee advanced on the Rangers, Alpha made the final adjustments on a special squirt gun in the Command Center. "This gun will really stick up that bee!" he said.

"Good work, Alpha," Zordon praised him. "Alert the Power Rangers!"

Alpha gave him a quick salute, then jabbed at the computer controls. "I'm sending you some back-up, Billy. It should even up the score!" He pressed more buttons, then shouted, *"Pasta la pizza baby!"* as the new weapon was teleported out of the Command

Center—and into the Blue Ranger's gloved hand.

"Thanks, Alpha!" the Blue Ranger said, climbing to his feet. "You sure did *your* homework!" Then he aimed the squirt gun straight at the Grumble Bee. "Here's the best lesson of all, you big buzz!"

CHAPTER 6

Billy fired both barrels of his new weapon and gooey liquid shot out. Alpha's special formula glommed on to the Grumble Bee's wings, making them too heavy to move. The sound waves stopped!

"The weapon worked!" Trini called.

"The bee's madder than a hornet," Billy joked as the furious Grumble Bee rolled on its back, trying to rub off the goo.

"Good job, dude," said Zack. "But are you okay? That venom nearly melted your suit."

Billy held his nose and nodded. "Aside from an aversion to the smell, I'm fine."

Jason drew out his special Power Sword and said, "Then let's finish the job, Power Rangers!"

The Power Rangers raced forward, their superweapons in hand, to defeat the Grumble Bee once and for all.

But evil Rita Repulsa, watching

from the moon, wasn't about to let that happen.

"Now my bee's small, but try fighting the beast *tall!*" she shrieked. With that, she hurled her magic staff toward the Earth. When the wicked wand hit the ground, the Grumble Bee expanded into a mega-monster.

The charging Power Rangers skidded to a stop when they saw that their enemy had grown ten times bigger.

Jason, the Red Ranger, thought fast. "We need Dinozord Power," he called to the others. "Now!"

The Power Rangers quickly called out their dinosaurs' names. "Tyrannosaurus!" "Pterodactyl!"

"Mastodon!" "Saber-toothed Tiger!" "Triceratops!"

Suddenly the ground trembled with the distant sound of dinosaur robots awakening.

Tyrannosaurus erupted from a steaming crack in the ground.

Mastodon broke through its cage of ice.

Triceratops charged across a scorching desert.

Saber-toothed Tiger leaped through a twisted jungle.

Pterodactyl erupted from the fires of a volcano.

Side by side the Dinozords raced like the wind to answer the call.

"Ready, everybody? Megazord

transformation," Jason shouted, activating his Power Crystal. "Power up!"

"We're on it!" the other Power Rangers yelled. "Locking in. On target!"

Two Zords locked into a third, *Clunk! Clang!* and became legs. Two more Zords locked in, *Clang! Thunk!* and formed arms.

The mighty head rose from its chest. Its helmet swung open and locked into place. Its shield clanged together to form the mighty Megazord!

The Power Rangers leaped into place in the control room behind the Megazord's flashing eyes.

The Megazord thundered forward to battle the Grumble Bee. The ground shook from the force of its movements. Its powerful fist slammed into the Grumble Bee. But the monster fought back. The two huge creatures struggled fiercely.

"I've had enough," Jason said from inside the Megazord cockpit. "It's time to finish that bully bee off for good. We need the mighty Power Sword!"

From the cockpit, the other Power Rangers shouted, *"Yes!"*

In a flash of lightning, the Power Sword swooped down from the sky. The mighty Megazord grabbed the weapon and took aim. It slammed the huge sword into the Grumble Bee.

Bolts of lightning zipped out of the blade, piercing the vicious beast. The monster sizzled and smoked—and turned to dust! The battle was over.

"Curses!" Rita screeched in her fortress on the moon. "I despise the Power Rangers! They give me such a headache!"

Goldar moved over to the telescope and shook his fist at the Power Rangers. "We'll be back!" the warrior promised.

The next afternoon at the youth center gym, Kimberly and Trini watched Jason and Zack practice karate. All of a sudden, Billy rushed up, a big grin on his face.

"I have outstanding news," he said. "I got an A-plus on the test and made the Young Scientists of America Club!"

His four friends gathered around to congratulate him.

"Morphinominal!" exclaimed Jason. "Your studying really paid off."

"You worked hard, Billy," Trini agreed. "You deserve it."

Billy's grin widened. "Thanks, guys," he said and admired the red A-plus Ms. Appleby had scrawled at the top of his paper. "I'm through battling *B's*—if you know what I mean!"

All the teens laughed.

"Let's celebrate at the snack bar," Kimberly suggested.

"Good idea," Jason agreed.

As the five teenagers headed into the lounge area, they spied Bulk and Skull sitting at a large table with stacks of books. Each had his eyes glued to a science book.

"What're you staring at?" Bulk snarled, looking up.

"One of the eight wonders of the world, I think," Jason said. "Are you two actually *studying?*"

Bulk curled his lip. "What's it look like, muscle head?" he asked. "Ol' Appleby said if I didn't get a C on the next test, she'd make the five top students tutor me every day this summer."

Zack looked around, counting his friends on his fingers. Suddenly, they all realized that *they* would be the ones tutoring Bulk—*all summer long!*

"Here, Bulk," Jason said, pulling up a chair. "Let me help you with that...."

Billy sat down next to them. "I can certainly teach you about science, Bulk. Anything you want to know."

"Yes," Kimberly agreed. "I think we can help you get that C *right away*."

Zack and Trini exchanged grins as they pulled up chairs.

Defeating the Grumble Bee had been hard enough. Teaching *Bulk* was really going to be a challenge!